Sister Secrets

Twink

Bimi

Pix

Sooze

Sili

Mariella

Kiki

Ivy

Book Nine

Sister Secrets

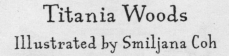

Titania Woods

Illustrated by Smiljana Coh

BLOOMSBURY

LONDON BERLIN NEW YORK

Bloomsbury Publishing, London, Berlin and New York

First published in Great Britain in 2009 by Bloomsbury Publishing Plc
36 Soho Square, London, W1D 3QY

This edition published in 2009

A CIP catalogue record of this book is available from the British Library

ISBN 978 1 4088 0494 0

FSC
Mixed Sources
Product group from well-managed
forests and other controlled sources

Cert no. SGS - COC - 2061
www.fsc.org
© 1996 Forest Stewardship Council

Typeset by Dorchester Typesetting Group Ltd
Printed in Great Britain by Clays Ltd, St Ives Plc

1 3 5 7 9 10 8 6 4 2

www.glitterwingsacademy.co.uk

For Antonia MacPhee –
Glitterwings' first and best fan

Chapter One

Twink Flutterby felt like singing as she and her mother skimmed over the top of the hill. How wonderful to be flying in the spring sunshine, with a brand new school year at Glitterwings Academy ahead of her!

Down below, Twink's little sister Teena was riding on Brownie, the Flutterby family's mouse. It was Teena's first term at Glitterwings, and Twink thought she looked just as excited and nervous as Twink had once felt.

But at least Teena had an older sister to show her

around. Twink felt very grown-up all of a sudden. It was her third year at Glitterwings, and she knew Teena would be looking up to her and asking for advice.

'Here we are!' said Twink's mother cheerfully as Glitterwings Academy came into view.

The massive oak tree stood in a field of yellow wild flowers, its new spring leaves green and curling. Tiny golden windows wound their way up its trunk, and the ornate double doors at its base stood open in welcome.

Good old Glitterwings, thought Twink. Oh, it was glimmery to be back! Then, remembering how she'd felt on *her* first day, she swooped down close to Teena.

'Just think,' she whispered in her sister's pointed ear, 'tomorrow you'll be sprinkled with fairy dust, and you'll be able to fly!'

Teena grinned at her. 'I know – I can hardly wait.'

Twink and her mother touched down on the front lawn. Crowds of returning students hovered about the tree like brightly coloured butterflies, shouting and calling to each other. Others stood chatting with their parents or checking in with their year heads. Teena, still perched on Brownie's glossy back, looked wide-eyed at the busy scene.

'Oh, Glitterwings is so lovely in springtime,' sighed Twink's mother, gazing up at the tree. 'I think it's my favourite term of all.'

Twink gave Teena a nudge. 'Get used to this – she says it every term!' she hissed.

Twink's mother overheard her and laughed. 'All right, clever-wings! Come along, Teena, let's tell Mrs Lightwing you're here. Twink, could you sort yourself out while I see to Teena?'

'Of course!' said Twink, pleased that her mother thought she was old enough to check in on her own.

She flew across to the third-year check-in area, beside one of the tree's roots. Her new year head was a tall, slender fairy called Miss Twilight. She had silver hair and purply-grey wings, and was the most exotic-looking teacher Twink had ever seen.

'You're in Violet Branch this year,' Miss Twilight informed Twink, ticking her off on a clover-leaf list. Her cobweb robes shimmered with tiny moonstones. 'And I'm going to be one of your teachers, so we'll be seeing a lot of each other.'

'Oh, which subject?' asked Twink eagerly.

'It's a new one,' said Miss Twilight with a mysterious smile. 'Miss Shimmery will be announcing it later!' She turned away to check in another student.

What could the new subject be? Lost in thought, Twink flew back to find her mother and Teena. She stopped short as she caught sight of a young first-year fairy waving goodbye to her parents. The fairy had bright purple wings, and *orange hair*!

Twink gaped. She had never seen orange hair on a fairy before – and this fairy's hair wasn't just orange, it was a brilliant, blazing orange, like firelight!

As Twink watched, the fairy dropped her hand with a sigh, and then noticed Twink observing her. A scowl creased her face. She snatched up her oak-leaf bag and stalked off.

Guilt pinched Twink's conscience. She hadn't meant to make the other fairy feel bad! Flying quickly over the grass, she landed beside her. 'I'm sorry I was staring,' she said earnestly. 'It's just that I've never seen hair the colour of yours before.'

The fairy's cheeks reddened. 'Isn't it awful?' she burst out. 'I'm the only fairy I know with orange hair.'

'It's not awful at all,' said Twink in surprise. 'It's really pretty – it's so different!' And it was: it framed the young fairy's face like dancing flames.

But the new girl grimaced in embarrassment. 'I don't want to be *different*. Everyone's always staring at me. I hate it!'

Twink held back a smile. The fairy sounded almost exactly like Twink's best friend, Bimi. Bimi had dark blue hair and silver and gold wings, and was extremely beautiful – but she hated being stared at, too, and had been very prickly when she and Twink had first met.

Impulsively, she offered her wing. 'I'm Twink,' she said. 'I'm in the third year.'

The fairy touched the tip of her wing to Twink's. 'I'm Summer,' she said, and smiled. 'Because when I was born, my mother said my hair was like a summer sunset!'

'It is!' laughed Twink. 'You're a first-year fairy, aren't you? I'll tell my sister, Teena, to look out for you. She's just starting school here, too.'

Summer's face lit up. 'That would be glimmery!' she said. 'I'm in Snowdrop Branch – I hope I get to meet her soon.'

Just then Mrs Lightwing, the first-year head, flitted over. 'Summer, there's a bird squad about to take some fairies up to Snowdrop Branch – you'd better go along with them, and choose your bed. Hello, Twink,' she added with a smile.

'Hi, Mrs Lightwing,' said Twink. She had been a bit afraid of Mrs Lightwing when she first met her, but had learned to like the gruff, no-nonsense teacher a great deal.

As Summer ran off Twink looked around for her mother and sister, and spotted them a short distance away. Mum was chatting to Miss Petal, the Flower Power teacher. Twink started across to them, eager to tell Teena about Summer.

But before Twink could reach Teena, another first-year fairy skipped across to her younger sister. 'Look, we're twins!' she cried. 'We've both got pink hair and lavender wings!'

The new fairy's long pink hair was pulled back with a clasp instead of worn loose, and her lavender wings were a touch darker than Teena's – but otherwise the two fairies looked very much alike.

'Ooh, we really are!' said Teena with a delighted grin.

'We'll have to be friends, then. Twins for ever!' laughed the other fairy, linking her arm through Teena's.

Twink blinked, hovering in place. Why, it was just like the first time she'd met Sooze! Sooze, a madcap fairy who Twink had been friends with since her first term, had declared herself Twink's *Opposite* when they first met, because of her lavender hair and pink wings.

'Twins for ever – that sounds familiar!' said a voice.

Turning, Twink saw that Sooze herself was fluttering beside her. 'Hello, Opposite!' she said, her violet eyes dancing. 'Isn't that your little sister?'

'Hi, Sooze,' returned Twink with a grin. 'Yes, she's called Teena – it's her first term here.'

Sooze chuckled. 'Well, guess what – her new "twin" is my cousin Zuzu! Isn't that funny? It looks like they're going to be friends, just the same as we were.'

'Glimmery!' exclaimed Twink. But as she glanced at Teena and Zuzu again, she felt a slight pang of foreboding. *Friends, just the same as we were . . .* What if that turned out to be true?

For although Sooze had been an exciting best friend at first, she hadn't turned out to be very dependable. In fact, when Twink had had so much trouble learning to fly, Sooze had quickly got bored with the problem, and had wounded Twink's feelings deeply.

Twink bit her lip. The last thing she wanted was

for Teena to get hurt.

'Um . . . is Zuzu very much like you?' she asked, trying to sound casual.

Sooze's eyebrows rose in surprise. 'I suppose so – I never really thought about it. Anyway, she's loads of fun. Oh, look, there's Sili. See you later, Twink!'

Twink winced as Sooze flew off. She knew all too well what Sooze's idea of 'fun' was! If Zuzu was even half as bad, then Teena would soon find herself being dragged into all sorts of scrapes.

Teena caught sight of her then, and the two young fairies came running over. 'Twink, this is Zuzu!' said Teena, beaming. 'And guess what? We're both going to be in Snowdrop Branch.'

'That's right – we're the terrible twins, together for ever!' put in Zuzu, leaning her pink head against Teena's.

'Oh,' said Twink weakly. 'That's great.'

The two girls looked even more alike than she'd first thought. Both had dark purple eyes, and were exactly the same size and height. Even so, Twink knew she could never mistake them. Zuzu's bright,

mischievous smile was just like Sooze's!

Zuzu tugged at Teena's hand. 'Come on, Twin – let's go and look at the inside of the school.'

'Glimmery! Bye, Twink,' called Teena over her shoulder as the two fairies ran off.

Twink sighed. She didn't have a good feeling about Zuzu at all! Why couldn't Teena have met Summer first instead? But at least the three fairies were all in Snowdrop Branch together. Maybe Teena would prefer Summer once she'd met the orange-haired fairy.

Twink's mother landed in a flurry of wings, with Brownie trotting behind on his lead. 'Has Teena gone into the school already? Let's catch up with her, so I can say goodbye to you both – my two Glitterwings girls!' She smiled fondly.

'OK,' said Twink. 'And listen, Mum, don't worry about anything. I'll take really good care of Teena this term, I promise.'

Her mother smoothed Twink's long pink hair. 'Yes, I'm sure that you'll help her out if she needs it. But she's grown up a lot in the two years since you've been at school, you know! Don't worry about Teena too much. I'd rather that you concentrated on your schoolwork.'

Twink hesitated, wondering whether to mention Zuzu. But it had been years since her mother was a student at Glitterwings, and she might not remember how important it was to have a best friend you could really count on.

She nodded reluctantly. 'All right, Mum.'

'That's my girl,' said her mother, giving her a warm hug. But as they flew off towards the school, Twink resolved that she *would* watch over Teena, no matter what her mother said – she had a feeling that her little sister might need it!

Chapter Two

Soon after Twink's mother left for home, the bird squad returned to the bottom of the tree. Teena and Zuzu mounted a pair of grey and yellow tits, perching on jaunty red saddles.

Twink hovered to one side. 'Would you like me to fly up to Snowdrop Branch with you?' she offered.

Teena looked surprised, and a little embarrassed. 'No thanks, Twink. I don't think any of the other girls are going up with their big sisters.'

'*Nobody* would – wasps, how awful!' shuddered Zuzu.

Twink's lavender wings tapped together in irritation, but she told herself to just ignore Zuzu. 'Well, make sure you hold on tightly,' she said to Teena.

The inside of Glitterwings Academy was like a high, golden tower, with corridors shooting off in all directions. Twink remembered the first time *she* had flown a bird up it – she'd been scared stiff!

'Twink, I *have* ridden on a bird before,' pointed out Teena, her cheeks turning pink. 'I'll be fine.'

'I know, but –' started Twink.

'Let's get going,' broke in Zuzu loudly. 'Snowdrop Branch!' she ordered, nudging her mount with her pixie boots. Twink darted back as the two birds took off in a rush.

'Wheee!' cried Zuzu, tipping her head back in the breeze.

'See you later, Twink!' called Teena. She waved over her shoulder with a grin.

Forcing a smile, Twink waved back. Her smile faded as she watched the two birds grow smaller, spiralling up the inside of the school. Oh, wasps – Zuzu was *exactly* like Sooze.

'Twink, there you are!' cried a voice.

Spinning about, Twink's face burst into a smile. 'Bimi!' she squealed. The two best friends hugged tightly, bouncing up and down.

'Are you in Violet Branch too?' asked Bimi excitedly.

Twink nodded, happiness flooding through her. Another year in the same branch together! 'Come on,' she said, grabbing her oak-leaf bag. 'Let's go and choose our beds!'

As the two fairies flew up the tree, Twink told Bimi about Teena and Zuzu. She had expected her best friend to be as concerned as she was, but instead Bimi's blue eyes looked puzzled. 'Well . . . what's the problem?' she asked.

Twink almost dropped her bag. 'Bimi! Don't you remember how badly Sooze let me down during our first term?'

Though Twink was still friends with Sooze — and had had some wonderful times with her in the past two years — she couldn't help feeling a sharp stab of hurt whenever she thought of how Sooze had treated her back then, when she'd needed a best friend so badly.

Bimi shrugged. 'Of course, but that doesn't mean that Zuzu would let anyone down. I think you should give her a chance.'

'I suppose so,' said Twink doubtfully, remembering Zuzu's cheeky smile.

'Besides, Teena seemed like an independent little thing when I stayed with you during the holidays,' added Bimi. 'I'm sure she can make up her own mind.'

Twink shrugged. Teena might like being independent, but that didn't mean she was always going to make good choices!

The two friends landed on the ledge in front of Violet Branch. A cluster of rich purple violets hung over the doorway, scenting the air. Twink pushed open the door – and forgot all about Teena for the moment. Their new branch was beautiful!

Violet Branch was a large, crooked branch filled with sunshine, with sleeping areas both on the main floor and in two loft spaces. A canopy of bright purple violets dangled over each mossy bed, and a carpet of green moss lay underfoot.

Twink and Bimi quickly took two beds in one of the lofts, side by side.

'Oh, this is lovely!' breathed Bimi, putting her oak-leaf bag on her bed. 'Look, we've got a window right over our beds!'

'It's glimmery,' agreed Twink, looking upwards. She could just imagine gazing out at the stars as she fell asleep.

Most of the other fairies had arrived by then as well, and there were squeals and hugs of welcome as Twink greeted old friends. Pix and Sili were in Violet Branch too, and Sooze and Kiki – and Mariella!

Twink blinked in surprise when she saw the pointy-faced fairy. Mariella had failed her Seedling Exams at the end of their second year, and Twink hadn't expected her to be in their class again.

Mariella blushed when she saw Twink looking at her. 'I took extra classes all through the holidays,' she explained stiffly. 'I passed in the end – I didn't

think I would, but I did!'

'I'm glad,' said Sooze, nudging her. 'I never thought I'd say this, but it wouldn't be the same without you, Mosquito Nose!'

Mariella pulled a face, but looked pleased anyway.

Zena was the only one of Twink's friends who was missing. 'She's in Pansy Branch this year,' said Sili glumly. 'Isn't it too bad, being split up after so long?'

Taking her place was a new girl called Ivy. Twink glanced at her curiously. Ivy had a tumble of curly light green hair, and white wings with swirling green markings. She was perched cross-legged on her bed, drawing something in a petal pad as the others chatted.

At first Twink thought the green-haired girl seemed a bit stand-offish, but then she suddenly looked up and smiled – and Twink knew that she was going to like Ivy after all.

With a *huff* and a *thump,* Mrs Hover, the matron, arrived, looking stouter than ever. 'Are we all here?' she asked, patting her bright pink hair. 'Lovely!

Come along then, girls – the opening session in the Great Branch is about to begin.'

Skimming to the door, the Violet Branch fairies took off into the trunk, joining the long line of fairies heading downwards towards the Great Branch. Bimi grabbed Twink's arm. 'Look!' she gasped, pointing.

Twink caught her breath. The new girl, Ivy, was chatting with another third-year fairy – who looked exactly like her! Twink stared from Ivy to the other girl in confusion. If they hadn't been wearing different leaf-dresses, she'd never have been able to tell them apart.

The fairies swooped into the Great Branch: a long, wide space with polished wood floors and rows of mossy tables. Over every table dangled a brightly coloured flower for each of the school's branches, so that the room looked like a cheerful, sunlit garden.

'Ivy, who's *that*?' demanded Pix as Ivy joined them. The other green-haired fairy flitted over to the Carnation Branch table.

Ivy laughed. 'That's Jade, my twin sister! We're identical.'

'Ooh, identical twins! That's so *interesting*,' breathed Sili as they all sat down.

Ivy looked surprised. 'Is it? I've always been one, so it just seems ordinary to me. I wish that Jade and I were in the same branch, though. We always were at our old school.'

'I suppose they want you to be your own fairy more, instead of just being a twin,' said Pix wisely.

Ivy pulled a glum face. 'Yes, but I *am* a twin. It's awful being on my own. Jade's my best friend.'

All the talk of twins and best friends reminded Twink of Teena. Twisting on her mushroom seat, she saw Teena and Zuzu sitting side by side at the Snowdrop Branch table, their pink heads bent together. Summer sat at the end, chatting to a fairy with yellow wings. As Twink watched another fairy leaned in, laughing at something Summer said.

Twink frowned. Summer looked as if she was getting on really well with the other girls in her branch. If Teena didn't make friends with her quickly, the bright-haired fairy would soon be best friends with someone else.

'Your attention, please,' called Miss Shimmery.

Twink turned with the rest of the school to face their HeadFairy. Miss Shimmery's rainbow wings glistened as she hovered at the front of the Branch.

'To all our returning students, welcome back!' she said in her low voice. 'And a very warm welcome to our new students, too.'

Twink listened attentively as Miss Shimmery

made her usual opening statements: school uniforms were required from the next day, the First Years would have Flight lessons first thing in the morning – delighted whispers swept through the First Years at this – and no high-speed flying was allowed in the school.

Peeking across at the Snowdrop table again, Twink smiled at the gleam in Teena's eyes. She knew that her little sister could hardly wait to fly.

Miss Shimmery pulled off her sparkle specs. 'Finally, I am pleased to announce that Glitterwings now has a star-gazing platform. Miss Twilight, our third-year head, will be teaching Star Magic to the Third Years and above.'

Star Magic! An excited murmur rippled through the Branch. Not many schools taught the subject, and it had a fascinating air of mystery to it.

So *that's* what Miss Twilight had been so secretive about! Twink's wings tingled as she glanced at her teacher, looking more exotic than ever in a shining purple cape. Oh, she was so glad she was a Third Year – she'd explode with curiosity otherwise!

Miss Twilight

Miss Shimmery scanned the school with a serious gaze. 'I must stress that although Star Magic is perfectly safe when you know what you're doing, it can be dangerous in inexperienced hands. Therefore, the star-gazing platform is strictly *off-limits* to our First and Second Years. Older students may only enter it during lessons; the door leading to the platform from the trunk will be locked at all other times. Is that clear?'

The school fell silent, staring solemnly back at her. A shiver ran down Twink's spine as she and

Bimi exchanged a look. No subject she'd ever taken had been *dangerous* before.

After a moment, the HeadFairy nodded. 'Good. In that case, I think it's time to eat. Butterflies commence!'

She raised her arm as she drifted back down to the platform. The doors to the Great Branch swung open, and a long stream of butterflies floated in, each carrying a platter of seed cakes or an acorn-shell pitcher of nectar.

'I wonder why First and Second Years can't take Star Magic?' said Kiki as a bright yellow butterfly served the Violet Branch table.

Mariella sniffed, helping herself to a seed cake. 'They're too young and silly, of course. It's *very* powerful magic. They'd get it all wrong, and who knows what might happen then?'

Sooze's eyes flashed wickedly. 'Unlike *you*, Mosquito Nose – you're so old and mature now, aren't you?'

Mariella stuck her tongue out at her as the others giggled.

'I bet she's right, though,' said Pix. 'Plus it's a night class. But wasps, remember when we were First Years? We didn't know *anything*!'

Twink slowly poured honey over her seed cake as the rest of the table carried on chatting. It was true, she realised. She had learned so much in the last two years! A lot of it was to do with her schoolwork, of course . . . but the most important things of all had to do with friendship.

She had been such a baby when she first started school at Glitterwings, thinking that the flashiest, most exciting friend was the best one. Tapping her wings together thoughtfully, Twink looked across at Teena and Zuzu again.

What sort of big sister would she be if she didn't try to help out, when she could see that Teena might be making a mistake? Why, how glimmery it would have been if *she'd* had a big sister to give her advice! Teena would probably be grateful to her for caring.

I'll have a word with her about Zuzu tomorrow, resolved Twink. *It can't do any harm – and it might do her lots of good!*

After dinner, the Snowdrop fairies waited outside the Great Branch for the birds that would fly them back to their own branch. Teena stared upwards, wondering where the star-gazing platform was.

'It sounds like just the place for a midnight feast, doesn't it?' she whispered to Zuzu.

Zuzu laughed. 'You heard what Miss Shimmery said – it's off-limits.'

'But that doesn't mean it really *is*,' said Teena with a grin. 'There must be a way to get in there.' She'd been listening to Twink's stories of midnight feasts and moonlit jaunts for the past two years. Now that *she* was finally at Glitterwings Academy, she meant to have some fun!

Zuzu adjusted the clasp that held back her long pink hair. 'I don't know, Teena,' she said doubtfully. 'There must be some reason why we're not supposed to go there.'

Just then the birds arrived, circling close to the ledge, and the subject was dropped for the time being. But as Teena climbed on to her bird, she looked upwards again.

A star-gazing platform. It sounded absolutely glimmery . . . and she had no intention of waiting for two years to see it!

Chapter
Three

Mrs Hover arrived at Violet Branch bright and early the next morning, bustling about as she made their new dresses with flashes of fairy dust. 'There you are, my lovely!' she exclaimed as she finished Twink's dress. 'And won't you look a treat in it.'

Putting on the dress, Twink had to agree. This was the prettiest uniform she'd had yet! The bright, rich purple of the violet petal dress suited her pink hair and lavender wings perfectly, while the yellow third-year sash was like a ribbon of sunshine around her middle.

'Glimmery!' said Kiki, adjusting her oak-leaf cap. 'But I thought we could make our *own* dresses this year.'

'Next year,' said Mrs Hover firmly as she put away her fairy dust. 'And that's still too soon, if you ask me! The things those fourth-year fairies try to get away with . . .' She shuddered. 'Now then, who wants timetables?'

Twink crowded around with the others as the rose-petal timetables were handed out. *Twink Flutterby, Third Year* said hers in silvery writing. She looked over it eagerly.

Introduction to Star Magic, Advanced Creature Kindness I (small mammals), Advanced Flower Power I (saplings and root systems), Weather Magic II, Advanced Fairy Dust I (practical applications), Dance III.

Nervous excitement fluttered through Twink. All of her classes sounded so grown-up! It was hard to believe that she was really in her third year, taking such difficult subjects.

'Advanced Creature Kindness,' murmured Bimi in

wonder, gazing down at her own timetable. 'Who would have ever thought it!'

Twink rubbed her wing against Bimi's. 'Me, that's who!' she grinned. The term before, her best friend had studied extremely hard to get into the advanced classes, and Twink was very proud of her – though not a bit surprised.

She *was* surprised, though, to find that Sooze was taking Advanced Fairy Dust. 'But you failed your Fairy Dust exam,' she said in confusion. 'How did you manage to get into the advanced class?'

Violet Branch stared as Sooze's cheeks turned pink – Sooze, who was never embarrassed in the least!

'I – er – took extra classes over the holiday, along with Mariella,' Sooze confessed. She smiled sheepishly. 'I suppose I didn't realise how much I liked working with fairy dust until I wasn't able to use it last term.'

'You had an easier time over the holidays than *I* did, though,' pointed out Mariella with a rueful smile. 'I had to practically redo the whole term, because I hardly studied at all last winter.'

Twink regarded them both with amazement. Fancy Sooze taking one of her classes seriously enough to pursue extra lessons in it – and Mariella actually keeping this fact a secret!

'All right, all right!' laughed Sooze, catching her look. Flitting across to Twink, she tugged her oak-leaf cap down her forehead. 'So I've grown up a bit – don't make a big wing-flap about it.'

As Violet Branch compared their timetables, Twink looked at the sun through the window. With a start, she realised it was getting late. 'I'm just going to dash over to Snowdrop Branch,' she said to Bimi. 'See you at breakfast!'

The tree trunk was quiet as Twink skimmed out of Violet Branch. Diving off the ledge, she glided gently down the tree.

Landing with a hop on the Snowdrop Branch ledge, Twink saw that a small flock of birds was already circling outside it, waiting to take the Snowdrop fairies to breakfast. Wasps, she'd better hurry!

'Teena!' she called, poking her head around the

doorway. The first-year fairies inside looked up in surprise.

Twink spotted her little sister standing beside a bed near the end of the row, tying her green first-year sash around her waist. Zuzu had the bed next to her, and was busy adjusting her oak-leaf cap to a jaunty angle.

'Teena!' Twink called again, more loudly. 'I need to talk to you.'

This time Teena heard. Her cheeks flushed slightly as she hurried over to the door. 'Twink, what is it?' she said.

Drawing Teena out on to the ledge, Twink lowered her voice. 'I just wanted to have a word with you about Zuzu,' she said.

Teena blinked. 'What about her?'

Twink took a breath. 'Well – I know how fun and exciting she probably seems, but that's not the most important thing, Teena.'

She quickly told her little sister about her own experiences with Sooze, and how she had learned that Bimi, though quieter and more thoughtful, was

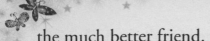

the much better friend.

Teena shrugged as she finished. 'OK. But what's that got to do with me?'

Behind them, the other fairies were starting to come out on to the ledge. The bird squad circled closer and landed in turn, so that each fairy could climb on to a saddled back and ride down to the Great Branch.

'Teena! Don't you see?' hissed Twink. 'Zuzu seems like a lot of fun, but she may not be the best friend for you.' She noticed Summer, smiling and chatting to the yellow-winged fairy. 'What about Summer?' she whispered. 'I met her yesterday, and she seems really nice.'

'She *is* nice,' said Teena in exasperation. 'That's not the point.'

'Of course it's the point!' exclaimed Twink. 'A best friend should be someone who –'

Teena's eyes flashed angrily. 'I *know* what a best friend is!' she said. 'And I'll choose my own, Twink. You don't even know Zuzu!'

'Teena, listen –' Twink started.

But Teena had already turned away and joined Zuzu in the queue. Zuzu leaned close, and looked as if she were asking a question. Teena's cheeks flared. She quickly shook her head.

A moment later, the two girls had climbed on to the last two birds and flown away. Twink felt a pang of hurt as she hovered in place, watching Teena grow smaller and smaller.

Her little sister didn't look back.

Thankfully, the morning passed in a whirl of lessons, so that Twink didn't have a chance to dwell on her row with Teena. For the first time, her branch wasn't taking every class together. It felt very strange and grown-up to be splitting up into smaller groups and going their own ways. And the lessons were all so advanced! Twink's head was spinning already, and it was only the first day.

Ivy was in several of Twink's classes, yet didn't appear at all worried by the difficulty of the lessons. Twink thought that the green-haired fairy almost seemed to live in a world of her own, always drawing in her sketch pad or gazing dreamily out of the window.

By lunchtime, Ivy had already been told off by two different teachers for not paying attention, and their Creature Kindness class had howled with laughter when she'd answered a question about *lice* instead of *mice*. Ivy herself had just smiled and shrugged, not bothered in the least.

'I like her,' Bimi said as she and Twink flew towards the Great Branch for lunch. 'She's as scatty as they come, but you couldn't meet a nicer fairy. And have you seen her drawings? They're *brilliant*.'

Overhearing them, Kiki swooped in close. 'Yes, I reckon we're lucky that we've got her and not her twin,' she said. 'Jade seems awfully quiet and serious!'

Twink started to respond, and then broke off as she spotted some first-year students flying up the trunk. 'Look, the First Years are flying!' she cried. 'I've got to go and find Teena.'

She jetted off, weaving her way through the streams of brightly coloured fairies. Her heart leapt as she spotted the white dresses of Snowdrop Branch. 'Teena, look at you!' she exclaimed, darting over to scoop her little sister into a hug. 'You're really flying!'

Teena's face shone. 'I know, isn't it great?' she squealed. She did a quick somersault, her lavender wings flashing. 'I love it!'

Twink smiled, relieved that Teena was too excited about flying to be very cross about their earlier row. 'Um, Teena, listen – about this morning –'

She broke off abruptly as Zuzu came skimming up. 'Look, we're even twins when we fly!' bragged Zuzu, linking her arm through Teena's. 'Aren't we glimmery?' She bounced wildly in the air, making Teena bounce as well. The two girls giggled.

Twink rolled her eyes before she could stop herself. Zuzu *must* have noticed that Twink was talking to her sister, but of course she'd just barged right in anyway!

Noticing Teena looking at her, Twink quickly tried to smooth her expression, but it was too late: Teena had seen her irritation at Zuzu. Her little

sister's face pinched into an accusing frown.

'Well, my *best friend* and I are going to go to lunch now,' said Teena pointedly. 'Goodbye, Twink.' And the two fairies flew off arm in arm, looking more like twins than ever.

Thinking that she'd try just once more, Twink attempted to talk to Teena again at dinner. Though she chose her words as carefully as she could, her little sister grew even angrier with her.

'Twink, give it a rest!' she exclaimed finally. 'I'll

choose my own friends – now just leave me alone!'
She flapped off in a huff.

Twink let out a breath. *Fine*, she thought. *I've
done my best – if Teena doesn't want to listen, that's her
problem!*

Later that evening, in the third-year Common
Branch, Twink tried to concentrate on her Flower
Power schoolwork: drawing an elaborate map of the
Glitterwings root system. But the memory of
Teena's furious gaze kept popping into her head,
and finally she put down her snail-trail pen and
slumped her chin in her hands.

All she'd wanted to do was help her little sister!
How had it gone so wrong?

'What's up?' said Bimi softly from the next mushroom desk.

Twink's wings grew warm. Remembering what
Bimi had said about giving Zuzu a chance, she had
an uncomfortable feeling that her best friend would
think she was in the wrong. 'Nothing,' she
muttered. 'I'm just tired, that's all.'

Bimi looked doubtful. 'Are you sure?'

She nodded, and Bimi shrugged and turned back to her own homework. Twink sighed. Bimi didn't have a sister, so she couldn't be expected to understand the worry that Twink felt over Teena.

She gazed at Ivy and Jade, who sat side by side at a pair of mushroom desks. As she watched, Ivy murmured a question to Jade, who whispered something back, leaning over to correct Ivy's page. The twins smiled at each other.

That was how sisters should be, thought Twink wistfully: friends who helped each other out. And that's all she'd been trying to do for Teena. She *knew* she was right about Summer being a better friend – but how could she make Teena see that when her little sister was so angry with her?

Suddenly she remembered something her father had said once about his work as a Fairy Medic. 'Just because you're right doesn't mean that anyone wants to hear it! Sometimes you have to choose tact instead if you want to help someone.'

Twink had asked him what he meant, and he'd explained that 'tact' was saying things in a way that other fairies wouldn't take offence at. 'It's no good being right if everyone wants to thump you for it, is it?' he'd added with a grin.

Maybe I wasn't very tactful, thought Twink now with a frown, tapping her wings together. *I'll try again later, once Teena's calmed down a bit – only next time I'll find a way to help her that won't get her wings in a twist!*

Chapter
Four

'Welcome to Star Magic,' said Miss Twilight with a smile, spreading her purply-grey wings. Sitting with the rest of the class in the warm spring evening, Twink gazed around her with shining eyes.

The star-gazing platform was an open, circular floor up at the very top of the tree. With no leaves to block the view, they seemed to be almost touching the millions of stars that glittered around them.

Miss Twilight hovered just above the wooden platform. 'As you all know, fairies draw energy from the sun, and we use this energy to perform all sorts of magic. However, there are other types of magic that we use starlight for, and –'

The door leading to the trunk flew open, and Ivy rushed out on to the platform. 'Sorry, Miss Twilight,' she gasped, clutching her sketchbook. 'I couldn't find the right branch.'

Miss Twilight shook her head. 'Take a seat, Ivy.'

Bimi and Twink glanced at each other in amusement as Ivy settled herself on the floor nearby, tumbling her belongings untidily around her. Couldn't find the right branch, when all you had to do was fly up to the highest point in the trunk and then go through the door? That was so like Ivy!

'Everyone, please take a moment to note the crystals,' continued Miss Twilight. Looking with the others, Twink saw nine pieces of quartz set around the edge of the platform, their facets gleaming in the starlight.

'The crystals help to strengthen the energy we get from the stars,' explained Miss Twilight. 'There's very powerful magic up here, and that's why it's important that only older fairies come on to the platform. Fairies who haven't been working with magic for very long can become dazzled by it – what we call *star-struck*.'

'What happens then?' breathed Sili, her eyes wide.

The tiny moonstones on Miss Twilight's robes twinkled as she moved. 'They often become dazed, and believe odd things. For instance, I once saw a star-struck young fairy who was convinced she was a duck!'

She smiled as the class burst into surprised giggles. 'But not all star-struck cases are so humorous,' she warned. 'I knew another fairy who thought she was in the middle of a snowstorm, even though it was high summer. She shivered so hard that she ended up in hospital for a week.'

Twink gulped. The class looked uneasily at each other, their laughter stilled.

'The truth is, you never know *what* being star-struck may do to a fairy – that's why it's such a dangerous condition,' continued Miss Twilight. 'However, it shouldn't happen to any of you, now

that you've been working with magic for two years.'

Twink let out a relieved breath. She'd been starting to wonder whether she even wanted to take this class!

'Now then,' said Miss Twilight. 'Does anyone know an example of a spell that we'd use Star Magic for?'

To no one's surprise, Pix's hand shot up. The red-haired fairy always knew the right answers, thought Twink. If she wasn't so nice, nobody would be able to bear her!

'Persuasion,' said Pix promptly. 'You can use Star Magic to persuade humans to do things, so long as it's not anything that will hurt them – like keeping them away from a forest, that sort of thing.'

Miss Twilight shook her silvery head. 'Not quite.'

Pix looked taken aback. 'Oh! But I thought –'

'Yes, Ivy?' said Miss Twilight. The green-haired fairy had put her hand in the air. The class stared at her in amazement. Ivy, volunteering to answer a question? She usually wasn't even *listening*!

'Persuasion is actually a Sunset spell,' said Ivy,

tucking back a strand of her curly hair. 'Star Magic spells are all about confusion: making things appear to be what they're not. Like casting a glamour, for example.'

'Very good!' beamed Miss Twilight. 'That's exactly right. Glamours, of course, are the spells that we fairies use to create illusions. Make sure that you read up on this tomorrow, Pix.'

There was silence as the class gaped from Ivy to Pix and back again. Twink held back a wild giggle. Pix looked as if she'd just swallowed a flea! Ivy, on the other hand, had gone back to drawing in her pad, humming happily to herself.

'Let me show you an example,' went on Miss Twilight, seeming not to notice the stir Ivy had caused. 'Mariella, please bring me a leaf from the supply cupboard.'

Mariella flew to the bark cupboard and brought out a brown, crumbling leaf. 'It's not in very good shape,' she said doubtfully, wrinkling her nose.

'That's all right – just put it there,' instructed Miss Twilight, indicating a space on the floor.

As the class craned to see, Miss Twilight raised her arms and shut her eyes. For a moment, starlight seemed to blaze around her like white flame, and then she pointed at the leaf.

Everyone gasped. Where the dead leaf had been there was now a sumptuous banquet of seed cakes, sparkling nectar and candied nuts. Twink's stomach rumbled as she gazed at it. She had never seen anything so delicious-looking in her life!

'Who'd like to have a taste?' asked Miss Twilight. There was a twinkle in her grey eyes.

Despite her longing to try the food, Twink hesitated. She knew it was only an illusion – but it looked so good! Her mouth watered as she imagined biting into the seed cake.

'*I* will!' said Sooze. She flitted to the front of the platform. As the class watched, she picked up a candied nut and popped it into her mouth. Her violet eyes widened. 'It's wonderful!'

Miss Twilight laughed. 'Yes, glamour food always is. But it doesn't nourish you, and if it was all you ate, you'd eventually die of starvation. Come on,

everyone, have a bite. It won't hurt you.'

Coming forward with the rest of the class, Twink cautiously tried a bit of seed cake. 'Oh!' she cried. It was even nicer than her gran's! Excited murmurs filled the platform as the fairies ate.

'That's enough,' said Miss Twilight after a few minutes. 'Take your seats. And now, you see again . . .' she waved her arm, 'what the food really is.' The dried leaf reappeared, now looking frayed and nibbled around the edges.

Twink stared at it in confusion. Somehow she had

forgotten that the food was only an illusion! From the startled faces of the fairies around her, she knew she wasn't the only one.

Miss Twilight chuckled. 'Glamour spells can be very convincing, can't they? So the first thing a student must learn is how to tell if something *is* under a glamour, or whether it's real. Open your petal pads, everyone.'

Twink picked up her snail-trail pen. Glancing at the dried leaf again, she couldn't imagine how she'd ever been taken in. Glamour spells must be extremely powerful magic!

The Star Magic teacher's silver hair shone in the moonlight. 'The first thing you must keep in mind is: *appearances can be deceptive.* Things are not always what they seem!'

Twink wrote the words down, and peered across at Ivy. Well, *that* was certainly true, she thought. Who would have ever supposed that Ivy would know the right answer instead of Pix?

The fairies chattered excitedly as they left the star-gazing platform, still abuzz from Miss Twilight's demonstration. 'Brilliant!' said Sooze as she swooped through the doorway that led back into the trunk. 'Imagine all the fun we'll have with magic like that –'

'Sooze!' said Pix in alarm. 'We're only allowed to take it because we're supposed to be sensible by now.'

Sooze grinned. 'Well, that doesn't mean we've all turned boring, does it? There must be *loads* of glimmery pranks we could play –'

Twink felt her heartbeat quicken despite herself. Nobody was quite as exciting as her Opposite! She understood all too well why Teena was attracted to Zuzu . . . but she had to make her little sister see what a best friend really was.

As Twink started down the trunk behind the others, she blinked in surprise. Why, there was Zuzu right there, half-hidden behind a knothole! The long pink hair and lavender wings were impossible to mistake.

No one else had noticed Zuzu, and ducking

around a bend in the trunk, Twink peered out with narrowed eyes. What was Sooze's cousin doing up here at this time of night? The only classroom this high up was the star-gazing platform . . . and Zuzu knew full well that she wasn't allowed on to it! As Twink watched, the pink-haired fairy darted out from behind the knothole and flew up towards the star-gazing door.

'Twink, aren't you coming?' called Bimi, fluttering far below.

Twink winced. *Not now!* she thought, glancing

down. When she looked back again, Zuzu was already skimming quickly away, diving down another fork of the trunk.

Frowning in thought, Twink spiralled down to where Bimi was waiting. Her best friend's gold and silver wings glinted as she hovered.

'What's up?' asked Bimi.

'I just saw Zuzu sneaking about,' said Twink slowly. 'She flew off when you called me.'

Bimi stared at her. 'Zuzu? What was she doing up here?'

'I don't know,' said Twink grimly. 'But I bet she was up to no good!'

Chapter Five

'Faster!' bellowed Madge from the side of the Fledge field. 'You lot are flying like you've got lead in your wings!'

Spurred on by the Fledge Captain's shouts, Twink *swooshed* through the centre pole as fast as she could, following the Flea. There he was, jumping overhead! Closer . . . closer . . .

From out of nowhere, Mia darted in and snatched him up. 'Ha! Just a second too slow, Twink,' she said, holding him over her head.

Twink wiped her damp forehead with a grin.

'Good move, Mia.'

Madge was shaking her head as the Fledge team flew off the field. 'You're all going to have to do better than that before our first game!' she called.

Despite the telling-off, Twink found herself smiling as she fluttered to the changing log with the others. She was a full member of the Glitterwings Fledge team this year, and it would take more than Madge's grumbling to take the shine off things.

Twink had been relieved when Fledge practice started, as it helped to keep her mind off Teena. Two weeks into the school year, Teena was still hardly speaking to Twink – and she and Zuzu were as close as ever.

Twink sighed as she towelled herself off and got changed. She hadn't seen Zuzu skulking about the star-gazing platform again, but she still couldn't shake the feeling that Sooze's cousin was trouble – and that her little sister was going to get hurt, somehow.

She closed the door to her bark locker. 'See you at the next practice, Twink,' said Mia, combing out her blue hair. 'Maybe Madge will have something nice to say by then!'

'Don't count on it,' said Twink with a smile. 'Bye, everyone!' She flitted from the changing log, still deep in thought. Suddenly she stopped in surprise. A fairy with bright orange hair was gliding slowly around the Fledge field. Summer!

'Hi, Twink,' said the first-year fairy as Twink came flying up. 'I saw you playing before – you got some great moves in!'

'Thanks,' said Twink in surprise. 'Do you like Fledge?'

Summer nodded enthusiastically. 'I love it! That was half the reason I was looking forward to flying – only then I found out that First Years can't try out for the team.' She made a face.

Twink laughed. 'I suppose they want you to get the hang of flying first. I could show you a few moves though, if you like.'

Summer's eyes lit up. '*Would* you?'

'Of course!' Swooping quickly to the ground, Twink put down her petal bag and then rejoined Summer. 'Have you done barrel rolls in Flight class yet? They're completely glimmery when you use them going through one of the poles – here, I'll show you!'

Half an hour later, the orange-haired fairy was speeding through the poles as if she'd been doing it all her life. 'It's too bad that you *can't* try out for the team this year,' Twink told her. 'You're a natural!'

'Really?' gasped Summer. 'Oh, I hope you're right! I want to play on the team next year more than *anything*.'

'Well, I bet you'll make it,' said Twink, flying down to collect her bag. 'You're even faster than Mia – and she's been playing for three years!'

The two fairies headed towards the school. The great oak tree sat on its hill, with the sunset blazing behind it. Twink hardly noticed. Summer was every bit as nice as she'd seemed that first day. Oh, *why* couldn't Teena have made friends with her instead?

She cleared her throat. 'Um, Summer . . . do you ever talk to Teena much?'

Summer shrugged. 'Not really . . . she and Zuzu always have their heads together.' She laughed. 'In fact, the rest of us are always teasing them – we say it's like they're busy plotting something!'

Plotting something? Twink frowned, remembering Zuzu sneaking about near the star-gazing platform.

'It's only a joke,' said Summer hastily, seeing Twink's expression. 'They just seem really close, that's all.'

'Mmm,' said Twink as they neared the double doors at the bottom of the tree. Maybe so, but she

still didn't trust Zuzu one bit! And it sounded as if Teena wasn't even *trying* to make friends with the other fairies.

All at once Twink saw how she could guide Teena in the right direction, without her little sister even realising it. 'Would you like to practise with me again sometime, Summer?' she asked. 'I know loads of other moves I could show you.'

'That would be *brilliant*!' exclaimed Summer.

'Great,' smiled Twink. 'How about tomorrow afternoon?'

'Teena, wait!' called Twink the next morning before breakfast, racing down the trunk to catch up with her. Oh, what luck! For a change, Teena was on her own.

'What?' asked Teena warily as Twink came speeding up. Twink thought her little sister looked cautious, as if she were afraid Twink was going to start lecturing her about Zuzu again. Well, no chance of that – this time she was going to see what a bit of tact could do!

'Nothing,' said Twink as the two sisters hovered beside a window. 'I just . . . I feel bad that we haven't been getting along, that's all.'

Her throat tightened. It was true – she had been so looking forward to being a proper big sister this term, and showing Teena around! And instead they were barely speaking.

Teena's expression softened. 'Oh, Twink, me too! I'm really sorry if I flew off the handle. It's just that Zuzu *is* my best friend, and that's all there is to it!'

'Of course,' said Twink. Quickly, she changed the subject. 'Teena, listen – would you like me to teach you some Fledge moves this afternoon?'

She held her breath as she waited for Teena's response. She knew how much her little sister liked Fledge – she'd been so excited when Twink was made a reserve for the team last year.

Teena's eyes widened eagerly. 'I'd love it! Can Zuzu come?'

Twink managed to hold back a groan. 'No, just you and me. I – I don't think I could show moves to more than one of you at a time. Besides, I want the two of us to spend some time on our own.'

Twink hardly ever lied, and to her own ears her voice sounded feeble and unconvincing. She was certain that Teena would become suspicious, but instead her little sister looked rather pleased. 'Oh! Well, all right. I'll meet you after lessons, then!'

Summer arrived at the Fledge field before Teena, dropping her petal bag on the ground and flying excitedly up to Twink. 'I've been looking forward to this all day!' she said. 'Thanks so much – it's really nice of you.'

'Oh, that's all right,' said Twink, feeling her pointed ears grow warm. Summer clearly had no idea that Twink had reasons of her own for wanting her here, and suddenly she felt rather guilty.

'We just need to wait for Teena,' she said. 'She's playing, too.'

Summer nodded unsuspectingly. 'OK – it'll be great to get some proper moves in! Does Teena like Fledge?'

'Yes, she loves it . . .' Twink trailed off as Teena herself came flying up. Her little sister's face was slack with disbelief as she stared first at Summer, and then at Twink.

'Hi, Teena,' said Twink with a bright smile. 'I, um – thought Summer could play, too. It's easier with three.'

'Oh, of *course*,' said Teena, crossing her arms over her chest. 'That's why you told me it had to be just the two of us!'

Twink's cheeks burned. 'I changed my mind, that's all. Come on – don't you want me to show you some moves?'

For a moment she thought Teena would refuse, but then her little sister let out a breath. 'Oh, all right! Hi, Summer,' she added grudgingly.

To Twink's relief, the two fairies were soon zipping about from one end of the field to the other, laughing and calling to each other. Her spirits lifted. It looked like her plan might work after all!

But the moment Summer headed back to school, Teena whirled round to face Twink. '*What* do you

think you're doing?' she demanded.

'Nothing!' spluttered Twink. 'I told you, I just –'

'*Ooh!*' Teena stamped her foot in the air. 'It's so obvious! You're still trying to get me to be best friends with Summer!'

'I am *not*,' cried Twink. 'And – and even if I was, well – why not? You won't listen to me about Zuzu, and –'

'You don't even know Zuzu!' shouted Teena. 'You think she's just like Sooze, but she's *not*.'

'Of course she is!' Twink yelled back, unable to hold it in any longer. 'Teena, *listen*. I saw Zuzu skulking about the star-gazing branch a few weeks ago, and –'

'*Zuzu?*' Teena's mouth fell open. 'But –'

'Yes, Zuzu!' said Twink. 'I don't know what she was up to, but it can't have been anything good. She's trouble, Teena – can't you see that?'

Teena stared at her. 'But . . . why do you think it was Zuzu?'

'Because she was wearing a Snowdrop dress, and had long pink hair and lavender wings!' said Twink

in exasperation. 'It was her, all right.'

To Twink's irritation, her little sister looked like she was about to burst out laughing.

'It's not funny!' she snapped. 'Teena, you really need to choose your friends better. I know you'd like Summer, if you just gave her a chance –'

Teena groaned loudly. 'Whatever you say, Sis! I've got to go now – Zuzu's waiting for me.' She flitted back towards the school in a flash of pink and white.

Oh! Twink huffed out a breath. Teena always thought she was right, no matter what anyone said. Well, Twink certainly wasn't going to try to help her again. Her little sister could find out about Zuzu on her own, the hard way!

Chapter
Six

'She did *what*?' Summer's surprised voice echoed through the first-year wash branch. A bit of moss she'd been using to scrub her arms lay forgotten in her hand as she stared at Teena.

Teena nodded crossly. 'She was trying to get us together, and make us be best friends! Can you believe it?'

'Oh.' Summer slowly started cleaning her arms again. 'I – I thought she was showing me Fledge moves because she liked me.'

Teena rolled her eyes. 'She *does* like you,' she

pointed out. 'She thinks you'd be the perfect best friend for me!'

'And I'm the worst friend in the world, apparently,' put in Zuzu dismally, combing her hair. Her lavender wings glinted in the steam. 'Teena, I still can't work out what I've done to make her hate me so much.'

Teena squeezed her best friend's arm. 'Don't worry about it. She's got it in her head that you're just like Sooze, and Sooze hurt her feelings once or something. *I* know you're not like that.'

Zuzu laughed suddenly. 'She doesn't seem to know *you* very well either, does she? Honestly – as if *I'd* ever be sneaking around the star-gazing platform!'

Teena grinned, fluttering her wings. 'Just wait – I *will* get you up there, and the others too, once I've worked out how to get in. It'll be the most glimmery place in the world for a midnight feast!'

'Well, what do we do in the meantime?' demanded Summer. Her orange eyebrows were drawn together in a hurt frown. 'I don't fancy Twink using me like that again. She could have *told* me what she was up to instead of being so sneaky.'

'I know,' said Teena sympathetically. 'She means well, but she still thinks I'm a baby who can't make my own decisions! We need to do something to show her how silly she's being about all three of us.'

Summer's eyes lit up. 'A prank!'

Teena felt a slow smile spread across her face. 'Ooh, yes! But nothing *too* bad – it has to be something that she'll laugh at afterwards. What do you think, Zu?'

Teena wasn't surprised to see a worried look appear on Zuzu's face. Though her twin could be outspoken and cheeky, deep down she was really a bit of a scaredy-fairy!

'Well . . .' said Zuzu, biting her lip.

Teena put an arm around her shoulders. 'Come on,' she wheedled. 'You hardly have to be involved at all. I think I've got an idea, and it'll be brilliant!'

Zuzu took a deep breath. 'All right,' she decided. 'I'm in!'

'And me,' said Summer with a grin. The three fairies touched their wings together. 'Let's show Twink what a moss brain she's being!'

'Even though it's underground, a tree's root system is really its heart,' said Miss Petal. She unrolled a large oak-leaf poster of the Glitterwings root system, pinning it up on the wall.

'So when you're working with trees, you must always take into account whether – *Ivy*!' Miss Petal interrupted herself with an exasperated sigh. 'Are

you listening to a word I'm saying?'

Ivy didn't look up. Sitting at the desk next to her, Twink saw that the green-haired fairy was drawing an elaborate picture of a water sprite sitting on a lily pad.

'Ivy,' she whispered from behind her hand. 'Miss Petal's talking to you!'

Ivy looked up dreamily. 'Hmm?'

'IVY!' bellowed Miss Petal. The class jumped. 'If you don't stop drawing and PAY ATTENTION, I'll send you out of this class!'

Ivy's eyes widened in surprise. 'Oh! Sorry, Miss Petal.' She calmly closed her sketch pad.

Twink shook her head in bewilderment. How could this be the same fairy who – just this morning in Creature Kindness – had argued with Pix about the care of moles, and *won*? It was as if Ivy lived on her own planet half the time, but could be the brainiest fairy in the school when she felt like it!

Glancing over at Pix, Twink saw the red-haired fairy gritting her teeth. Ivy's occasional bursts of brilliance must be driving her mad. Pix was used to being the cleverest fairy in their year – it had to be annoying to be shown up by a scatterbrain like Ivy.

The magpie's call echoed through the school, signalling the end of lessons for the day. Twink gathered her things together. Beside her, Ivy was packing up her petal bag, humming to herself.

'Ivy, wait!' called Twink as they flitted from the classroom. She caught up with the green-haired fairy and cleared her throat. 'I just wanted to ask you – I mean . . .'

'What?' Ivy's eyes were wide and innocent, but there was a faint spark of mischief in them, too. Suddenly Twink wondered whether Ivy was *quite* as dreamy as she sometimes made out!

She smiled despite herself. 'Well . . . it's just that sometimes you seem . . .'

Twink broke off as Summer came flying up, panting and out of breath. 'Twink! I've been looking *everywhere* for you,' she cried. 'I need to talk to you – it's really important.'

'I'll go and find Jade, then. See you later, Twink!' said Ivy.

After Ivy had fluttered off, Twink quickly drew Summer to a small window seat set high up in the tree's trunk. 'Is something wrong?' she asked anxiously.

Summer nodded her orange head. 'Twink, remember when I said that we sometimes tease Zuzu and Teena about plotting something?'

Dread shivered across Twink's wings. 'Yes – what about it?'

Summer's hands twisted in her lap. 'Well, it turns out it *wasn't* a joke, at least not about Zuzu. Oh, Twink, I found out that she's been plotting an awful, awful prank – and Teena refused to believe me! She thinks Zuzu's just perfect.'

Summer quickly told Twink what Zuzu was planning. Twink gasped in alarm. 'But she *can't*! You could all get into real trouble for that.'

Summer looked close to tears. 'I know! The rest of us have tried to talk her out of it, but she just won't listen. Can't you stop her, Twink? Please? You're the only one I can ask.'

'I'll go and have a word with her right now,' said Twink. Her jaw felt stiff and angry. Oh, that Zuzu! Twink had known she was trouble, but nothing like *this*. Why, the Snowdrop Branch fairies could all get expelled!

'No, don't!' burst out Summer. 'I mean – I mean, she'd be furious if she knew I'd told you. Can't you catch her in the act, somehow?'

Twink considered it, tapping her wings together. 'Maybe that *would* be better,' she said. 'I could really frighten her, so that she won't do it again.'

Relief shone on Summer's face. 'Oh, good! That's the best way, I'm sure of it. Zuzu's planning on getting the fairy dust tonight, after glow-worms out.'

'Well, she won't get very far – I'll be waiting for her!' said Twink. She felt a twist of satisfaction. It would be glimmery to actually catch Zuzu out, and prove to Teena how right she'd been about her new best friend. Maybe now Teena would actually listen to her!

* * *

That night Twink sat on her mossy bed in her cobweb nightgown, polishing her lavender wings until they gleamed. On the bed beside her, Bimi was studying her Creature Kindness book as she combed her dark blue hair.

Twink sighed. She wanted *so* much to tell Bimi about Zuzu's scheme, but she knew her best friend still wasn't convinced that Sooze's cousin was really that bad. Wouldn't it be better to wait until she had the evidence, and *then* tell Bimi everything?

Looking up, Bimi caught the expression on her face. 'Twink, something *is* wrong, isn't it?' she asked, closing her book.

Twink hesitated as she put her wing polish away. 'Not really,' she said. 'I mean . . . well, there *is* something, but I'll tell you later.'

Bimi's pretty face creased in concern. 'Are you sure? Why can't you tell me now?'

'I just can't,' said Twink. 'Trust me, Bimi – I'll have loads to tell you tomorrow!'

After glow-worms out, Twink waited until she

heard slow, steady breathing all around her. Carefully, she slipped out of bed. Pulling on her dressing gown, she glided down to the main floor of the branch.

Sooze slept there, and Twink glanced at her sleeping figure, wondering what she'd say when she found out about Zuzu's scheme. It should really be *Sooze* stopping her cousin, realised Twink suddenly. Why had Summer asked her to do it?

Twink's pink eyebrows drew together, and then she shrugged. It must just be that Summer didn't know Sooze. In any event, Sooze would be furious when she found out. Even *she* wouldn't attempt a prank as daft as the one Zuzu was planning!

Twink fluttered up to unhook a glow-worm lantern from the ceiling, and then tiptoed on to the ledge and shut the door softly behind her. It was so dark! But she couldn't use her lantern yet; Zuzu might see her.

Taking a deep breath, Twink dived off the ledge and skimmed downwards, towards the bottom of

the tree. When she reached the supplies branch, she crouched under the shadowy ledge, keeping out of sight.

Nothing happened for what seemed like ages. Twink bit her lip worriedly. Had she missed Zuzu somehow? But then she heard the faint stirring of wings. She peeked out, her heart thumping hard.

Even in the dim light, Twink could see that the fairy landing on the ledge had long pink hair pulled back in a clasp, and wore a Snowdrop dressing gown. As Twink watched, Zuzu eased open the door to the supplies branch and vanished inside.

Twink waited for several moments, trembling with expectation. *Now!* she thought, and swooped into the supplies branch. 'Glow-worms on!' she shouted. 'Stop right there, Zuzu!'

The pink-haired fairy was standing near a bag of fairy dust, her back to Twink. To Twink's surprise, she didn't spin around to see who had spoken – instead, she quickly grabbed up some fairy dust and rushed to the window.

'Hey, wait!' called Twink. 'Where do you think you're going?'

Zuzu didn't bother to answer. Deftly, the cheeky little fairy undid the catch and shot outside!

Jetting across the branch, Twink squirmed through the window after her. She could just see the outline of a fairy soaring upwards through the night, heading for Snowdrop Branch.

Twink sped after her, but Zuzu had had too much of a head start. Twink clenched her fists as she watched the younger fairy do a barrel roll. A taunting giggle floated through the air.

Oh! Just wait until she got her hands on her – Zuzu wouldn't be laughing then! Twink raced even faster, whipping past leaves and branches. Still chortling, Zuzu dived towards Snowdrop Branch and disappeared through an open window.

Ha! I've got her now! thought Twink. She zoomed towards the branch, already planning exactly what she was going to say to the wayward fairy. She could hardly wait!

'WHAT do you think you're doing?' boomed a voice.

'Aargh!' cried Twink, skidding to a mid-air halt. Whirling about, her eyes widened in horror. Hovering just above her was Mrs Lightwing, the first-year head!

The teacher flew slowly forward until she was only a wing's length from Twink. Her face was stormy. 'Good evening, Twink. Can you explain what you're doing out here in the middle of the night?'

'I – um –' Twink glanced desperately at Snowdrop Branch, several branches above them. Its windows were dark.

'I'm waiting, Twink.' When she didn't reply, Mrs Lightwing shook her head. 'I would have thought that you're a bit old to be playing pranks now, my girl! If you can't explain yourself, then –'

'But it wasn't me, it was Zuzu!' burst out Twink. Then she caught her breath in alarm. What had she done? It was an unwritten rule at Glitterwings that one should never be a tell-tale.

'*Zuzu?*' Mrs Lightwing stared at her. 'What are you talking about?'

Twink gulped miserably. But having said this much, she knew she might as well say the rest. 'I – well – you see, she was planning this terrible prank, and I was just trying to stop her.'

'Go on,' said Mrs Lightwing, raising one sky-blue eyebrow.

Twink cringed. To be honest, she was a bit frightened to even *tell* Mrs Lightwing what Zuzu had been plotting. 'Well – she stole some fairy dust, and then she was going to sneak into your room while you were asleep, and – and put a power spell on you, so that you had to do everything she said.'

Mrs Lightwing gaped at her. 'A *power* spell? On *me*?'

Twink nodded. 'She – she sneaked into the restricted section of the library to find out how to do it. She thought it would be funny.'

For a moment, Twink actually thought the first-year head was trying not to smile. Then her eyes narrowed. 'Are you saying that you were trying to stop Zuzu just now?'

Twink hesitated, wondering why Mrs Lightwing looked so suspicious. 'Yes, she had just come out of the supplies branch, and –'

'Stop right there!' ordered Mrs Lightwing. 'Twink, Zuzu is in the infirmary tonight with a bruised wing – I've just come from checking on her. There is no way that you could have been following her.'

'But I was! I saw her!' cried Twink.

'Enough,' said Mrs Lightwing crossly. 'I've heard through the grapevine that you don't like Zuzu, but I wouldn't have thought this of you, Twink – trying to get a younger student into trouble! Now, if you can't explain why you're really out here, then I'll have no choice but to punish you.'

'But . . . that *is* why I'm out here,' whispered Twink. Hot tears pricked at her eyes. 'Mrs Lightwing, I promise I saw Zuzu – just go into Snowdrop Branch and see for yourself!'

'I'll do better than that!' snapped Mrs Lightwing. 'Come with me, Twink.'

Grimly, Mrs Lightwing led the way back into Glitterwings, using the teachers' entrance midway up the tree. A few moments later, she was holding up a lantern in the infirmary. Twink stared down in confusion at Zuzu's sleeping form.

'But – but it *was* her,' she repeated miserably once they were outside the infirmary again. 'I don't know how she did it – maybe she doubled back really quickly, or –'

Mrs Lightwing's eyes flashed in the lantern-light.

'Quiet!' she barked. 'I've heard more than enough, Twink. Get back to bed this instant! And tomorrow you're to do a hundred lines for me: *I must not sneak about and tell lies!*'

Chapter
Seven

'But if it wasn't Zuzu –' started Bimi.

'It *was*!' said Twink hotly, putting down her snail-trail pen. The two friends were sitting in the library as Twink did her lines. High above, students skimmed about the tall shelves like hummingbirds.

'Bimi, I saw her!' insisted Twink. Glancing at Mrs Stamen, she lowered her voice. 'She was right there, plain as day. Why, she probably had the whole thing planned, just to get me into trouble.'

Bimi made a face. 'Why would she do that?'

'Because she knows I don't like her!' Twink

stopped short, staring at Bimi. 'You don't believe me, do you?'

Bimi rubbed her wing against Twink's. 'It's not that! It's just – well, I wonder if there could be some mistake.'

'*What* mistake?' said Twink in exasperation. 'Summer *told* me what Zuzu was going to do, and then later on that night there she was, doing it!'

'Only it wasn't her,' pointed out Bimi.

'It *was*! I saw her.' Twink propped her chin on her hand, her thoughts spinning in angry circles. She knew it had been Zuzu – and yet somehow it hadn't been! Was she going mad?

'Saw who?' asked a voice. Looking around, Twink saw Ivy hovering nearby. The green-haired fairy flitted over and sat down at their table, tucking her wings behind her back.

'Who did you see?' she asked again, glancing from Bimi to Twink.

Twink shrugged. She liked Ivy, but she didn't know her very well yet – and it seemed a bit pushy of her to sit down with them uninvited!

Ivy put her hand on Twink's arm. 'Please tell me,' she said. 'I overheard a bit, and – well, I have a reason for asking! Just trust me, all right?'

And all at once, Twink found that she *did* trust her. Taking a deep breath, she related the whole story – from her first meeting with Zuzu to the disastrous events of the night before.

To her amazement, Ivy burst out laughing. 'Oh, they got you!'

'What do you mean?' demanded Twink. *What* was so funny? Beside her, Bimi looked just as confused as she felt.

Ivy smiled. 'Well, they call each other *twins*, don't they? And they look alike, you said so yourself! It's easy – they just switched places. Jade and I do it all the time.'

'*Switched places?*' Twink gaped at her. 'But –'

'Of course!' Ivy fluttered her green and white wings. 'Why, *you* almost guessed the other day about me and Jade. We swap lessons sometimes. It's easy! We just meet up beforehand, switch our dresses, and there you go.'

Bimi looked dazed. 'But – that's cheating.'

Ivy's eyebrows shot up. 'No, it's not. We never take exams for each other. It's only for a joke – and hasn't it been glimmery?' Her green eyes sparkled. 'Especially seeing Pix try to work it out! She doesn't know whether she's coming or going.'

A startled laugh escaped Twink despite herself. 'Ivy! Is *that* how you – I mean, how Jade always knows all the answers? Because she's taken the class before?'

'Partly,' said Ivy with a grin. 'But she really is very clever, too.'

Bimi clapped a hand over her mouth as she giggled. 'Oh, poor Pix! She's been going *mad.*'

'Well, don't say anything,' said Ivy. 'Everyone will realise what's going on soon enough, and we want to have fun for as long as we can. Especially Jade. She's usually so serious that it's a real laugh for her!'

'We won't tell – will we, Twink?' promised Bimi.

Twink nodded. 'Your secret's safe with us, Ivy! Though I don't know how we'll keep from laughing the next time Jade knows all the answers in class.'

Then her smile faded as her thoughts returned to Teena. 'So you think – you think it was really *Teena* I saw?' she said slowly.

'Definitely,' said Ivy. 'Think about it – you only saw her in shadow, and the back of her head. So how did you know it was Zuzu?'

'Because . . . she was wearing Zuzu's hair clasp,' said Twink feebly. Oh, it seemed so obvious now! No wonder the fairy hadn't turned to face her. It had been *Teena*!

'There, you see?' said Ivy. 'She knew you'd think she was Zuzu, because she was *supposed* to be Zuzu – and then your mind filled in the rest!' She bounced up from the table. 'Anyway, I'm meeting Jade at the tuck shop. Remember your promise, you two, all right?'

Twink and Bimi agreed – and then glanced at each other worriedly as Ivy flew from the library.

'So it was Teena!' breathed Bimi. 'But why would she do such a thing?'

Twink's chest felt tight. 'I bet Zuzu put her up to it – and Summer, too, for that matter. Zuzu probably planned the whole thing! And Teena went along with it.' Pulling the petal towards her again, Twink started scribbling lines as fast as she could.

'But Twink, you don't *know* that,' protested Bimi. 'I think you should talk to Teena, and find out what really happened!'

Her best friend had a point. Twink looked down, playing with her snail-trail pen. 'All right, I'll talk to Teena,' she said finally. 'Maybe – maybe there's some explanation.'

But she didn't believe the words, even as she said them. Teena had pretended to be Zuzu just to get Twink into trouble. Hurt anger stuck like a stone in Twink's throat. How could her sister explain *that?*

'Oh no!' gasped Teena in dismay. 'Is that why you didn't follow me into Snowdrop Branch? We didn't know what had happened!'

'So it *was* you,' said Twink bitterly. It pained her to have Teena admit it, even though she'd known it must be true.

The two sisters were hovering outside the main

entrance to the tree, where Twink had caught up with Teena after Flight class. Teena nodded, hugging her petal bag. 'It was only meant to be a joke, Twink!'

Twink stared at her, hardly able to believe her ears. 'A *joke*? To have Mrs Lightwing catch me?'

'No!' cried Teena. 'We didn't know she would. We just thought you'd come in the window after me, and then you'd see that Zuzu wasn't even *there*, and you'd realise –'

'What?' burst out Twink. 'That she's a really bad influence on you? Because she *is*, Teena – I've never known you to act this way before!'

Teena's eyes grew wide. 'But – but I didn't do anything really bad,' she whispered. 'Neither did Zuzu. We just wanted to show you that –'

Deep down, Twink knew she should listen to what her little sister had to say. But then she thought of Zuzu's smug, cheeky face, and she felt on fire. Oh, Zuzu must be having a great time sniggering at Twink now! And here was Teena *defending* her.

'Well, don't worry, Teena – I've had enough of

trying to help you!' she interrupted coldly. 'You and your precious Zuzu can *stay* friends, for all I care!'

'But you don't understand!' wailed Teena, her eyes bright with tears. 'It was *my* idea, not –'

Twink didn't hear. She had already flown back into the school, her pink hair whistling behind her.

Teena hovered by herself, staring after Twink. She couldn't blame Twink for being angry about the

lines, but she hadn't even given Teena a chance to explain! She'd just stormed off without listening.

Shakily, Teena wiped her eyes. Well, if Twink had had enough, then *she* had, too! She needed something to take her mind off things – and all at once she knew just the thing.

Swallowing hard, Teena gazed up at the top branches of the tree. She couldn't see it from here, but she knew the star-gazing platform was up there, waiting for her.

A sudden idea popped into Teena's head, and she caught her breath. Why had she wasted so much time trying to get to the platform from inside the school? All she had to do was climb out of the Snowdrop branch window, and fly right to it!

Her hands felt clammy, and she wiped them on her skirt. Though she hadn't admitted it to Zuzu, the thought of actually going up there made her a bit nervous. Was it really dangerous, like Miss Shimmery had said?

Then Teena remembered Twink's angry face, and her resolve hardened. Well, she didn't care. She

would go up there, no matter what – and that very night, too!

'Twink? Twink, wake up!'

'Um?' Twink stirred drowsily, cuddled into her petal duvet.

'Twink! *Please* wake up; you've got to!' The fairy shaking her sounded close to tears.

This time the words reached her, and Twink sat up in bed, blinking. What was going on? What time was it? Then she saw who the fairy at her bedside was, and she stiffened.

'Summer! What are *you* doing here?'

The younger fairy's tear-stained face gleamed in the moonlight. 'It's – it's Teena and Zuzu,' she choked out. 'They've gone up to the star-gazing platform, only that was ages ago, and they're not back yet!'

In the next bed, Bimi propped herself up on one elbow, listening.

Twink snorted. 'Oh, right! And I suppose when I fly up there, it won't be Teena and Zuzu at all, will

97

it? Then Mrs Lightwing will catch me, and –'

'No!' said Summer. 'It's true, I promise! She's been wanting to go up to the star-gazing platform for ages, and tonight she said she was going no matter what, and then they *both* went, because –'

'Hang on – you mean they're *really* up there?' cried Twink. Fear shivered through her as she recalled Miss Twilight's description of star-struck fairies.

Summer nodded, gulping hard. 'Can't – can't you help, Twink? We're all so scared – we don't know why they're taking so long –'

Twink leapt out of bed. Grabbing her dressing gown, she pulled it on with shaking hands. 'Bimi, go and get Miss Twilight!' she said urgently.

Bimi was already out of bed, shrugging into her own dressing gown. 'I'll be as quick as I can!' she said, her face pale. Her bright wings glinted as she sped from the branch.

'Sooze!' hissed Twink, gliding down from the loft space. 'Sooze!'

'Mmf?' muttered Sooze, lying on her stomach.

Twink shook her shoulder. 'Sooze, wake up! You've got to help. It's that cousin of yours – she's taken Teena up to the star-gazing platform! Bimi's gone to get Miss Twilight, but we've got to hurry!'

Chapter Eight

At first the star-gazing platform had been fun.

Once Zuzu saw that Teena was determined to fly up there, she'd taken a deep breath and insisted on joining her – because what if it really *was* dangerous? Her twin shouldn't be going alone if that were the case.

So, pushing aside her fears, Zuzu had squirmed out of the Snowdrop Branch window after Teena. Spreading her wings, she bobbed in the air, feeling exhilarated by the warm spring night despite herself.

'Isn't this glimmery?' Teena whispered over her

shoulder as they fluttered upwards. There was a full moon, looking like a huge, silvery eye peering through the tree's branches.

Zuzu had to agree. Her heart sang as they reached the top of the tree. She'd never flown so high before! It was dizzying and exciting and wonderful, all at the same time.

'There it is!' hissed Teena.

Following her best friend's pointing finger, Zuzu's pulse skipped a beat. The star-gazing platform lay just below them, like a circular raft floating atop a sea of branches.

Teena touched down on the centre of the platform, looking happily around her. 'Oh, isn't it *wonderful*! I can hardly wait to get everyone up here for a midnight feast.'

Landing beside her, Zuzu peered at the nine crystals that glowed around them. Their light seemed weird and unearthly, and Zuzu bit her lip. 'Teena, we won't stay long, will we?'

'No, of course not! I just wanted to see it.' Sitting cross-legged on the floor, Teena smiled up at the stars.

Sitting beside her, Zuzu felt herself relax. It *was* wonderful to be up here with her best friend, with the crystals gleaming so brightly. Her thoughts began to drift as she gazed at them. Why had they made her nervous? They were so pretty, like lanterns . . . like white fire . . . like shining gems . . .

All at once Zuzu blinked, starting awake. How long had they been up here? It seemed like just a heartbeat, but the moon had moved – hadn't it? She shook her head dazedly, feeling rather frightened.

Suddenly Teena started to giggle.

'What is it?' asked Zuzu. A smile grew across her own face, though she wasn't sure why.

Teena laughed harder, clutching her ankles and rocking back and forth. 'Oh!' she spluttered. 'It's so funny! I'm – I'm a flower!'

'A *flower*?' Zuzu stared at her as the bright light from the crystals shone around them. But somehow the notion didn't seem so strange. She and Teena *could* be flowers, she realised. Why, their legs were just like stems! And their wings just like petals!

Zuzu began to laugh. 'What – what kind of flower?'

'I'm a daisy!' shrieked Teena. 'And you – you're an *apple blossom*!'

This seemed the most marvellous thing Zuzu had ever heard. She jumped to her feet. 'Look at me!' she said, spreading her arms. 'I'm an apple blossom, dancing in the wind!'

Teena joined her, and in no time at all the two fairies were capering about the platform, fluttering their wings and giggling.

'Ooh!' cried Teena, stopping short. 'Do you know what flowers can do?'

'What?' asked Zuzu eagerly.

'We can float on the breeze!' announced Teena. She sprang on to the platform railing, swaying a bit. 'Come on, Twin! Let's float down to the ground! Flowers don't even need wings!'

'Float?' The idea was delightful. Zuzu jumped up next to Teena, peering downwards. Then she frowned. What looked like a whole forest of branches lay between them and the ground.

'But . . . won't we hit a branch?' she asked doubt-fully. She had a vague feeling that there was something wrong with their plan, though she couldn't imagine what. Something . . . something they hadn't thought of . . .

'Of course not!' Teena's eyes sparkled in the crystal light. 'Flowers *drift*. We'll drift right around them.'

'Oh!' said Zuzu, greatly relieved. *That* explained it. She grinned. 'Well, what are we waiting for?'

Teena grasped her hand tightly. 'Come on, then – on the count of three!'

The two friends stood side by side, holding hands as they teetered on the slender railing. 'One,' they chanted. 'Two . . .'

Squeezing quickly through a window, Twink and Sooze sped upwards, dodging leaves and branches as they flew.

Fear pounded through Twink like a raging water-fall. Oh, what if something had happened to Teena? She'd never forgive herself for not looking after her sister better.

'Come on, Sooze, faster!' she called as they neared the top of the tree.

'Oh, wasps – look!' shouted Sooze, pointing.

Twink held back a shriek. There were Teena and Zuzu, standing on the railing of the star-gazing platform – with their wings folded behind their backs!

'What are you doing?' yelled Sooze frantically. 'Get down, the pair of you!'

Zuzu blinked, wavering. Suddenly she cried out and flung her arms around Teena. Teena struggled with her, arms flailing. The two fairies stumbled, and Twink gasped. Zuzu was clearly star-struck – and was trying to push Teena over the edge of the platform!

Her pulse roared through her brain. '*Get away from my sister!*' she screamed.

Jetting to the platform, she snatched Teena off the railing and into the air. Dimly, she was aware of Zuzu falling backwards as Teena squawked in surprise, kicking and squirming in Twink's arms. 'Let me go! Let me –'

'Stop it!' yelled Twink. She swerved narrowly past

a branch, trying to land them both safely. 'Teena, we'll –'

Crash! The two fairies were thrown apart as they slammed into a branch. Twink slumped against the rough bark. Oh, her head!

Beside her, Teena was huddled against a fork in the branch, crying softly. Ignoring her throbbing skull, Twink crawled over and touched her shoulder. 'Teena?' she whispered.

'What happened?' sobbed Teena. 'I don't under-stand . . . Twink, I'm so confused!' She flung herself into Twink's arms, and the two sisters hugged tightly. Twink's heart was hammering. Oh, if anything had happened to Teena!

She smoothed her sister's long hair. 'Hush, it's all right,' she soothed. 'I've got you.'

Gulping and sniffling, Teena sat up. 'What – what happened?' she asked.

'Zuzu tried to push you over the edge of the plat-form,' said Twink, glaring upwards. She could hear Zuzu crying, and Sooze talking softly to her. Good! She was glad that Sooze's cousin was so upset.

Teena's mouth dropped open. 'No, she didn't.'

'She *did*,' said Twink. 'Teena, I saw the whole thing – you were both on the edge, and –'

'No, I remember now!' cried Teena. 'It was like we were under a spell! I thought we were flowers, and that we could drift to the ground – and then Zuzu broke out of it, and she was trying to *stop* me.'

Twink's jaw tightened. She thought if she heard Zuzu's name once more, she'd scream! 'Teena, *when* are you going to stop defending her? You wouldn't even have been up here if it weren't for her!'

'I think it's the other way around, *actually*,' announced a voice. Sooze fluttered down to Twink's branch, her arm firmly around the sobbing Zuzu. 'Twink, what's been going on this term? Zu says you hate her!'

Twink flapped her wings angrily. 'I don't *hate* her – but it's obvious what sort of fairy she is, isn't it? Teena never got into a wing's breadth of trouble before, and now –'

'Now *what*?' Sooze stared at her. 'You can't be suggesting that this was *Zuzu's* fault – she'd never do something like this on her own!'

Zuzu sobbed harder, covering her face with her hands. 'I only wanted to help – I –'

'Ha!' shouted Twink. The leaves trembled around them. 'For your information, I saw her up here *weeks* ago, sneaking around, and –' Suddenly Twink remembered the prank that had been played on her, and she stopped in confusion. *Had* it been Zuzu she'd seen that day? Or –

'You're not listening! You never listen!' screeched

Teena, stamping her foot. '*I'm* the one who wanted to come up here, not Zuzu. It was me you saw! That's why we played the prank on you – to show you how wrong you've been about everything!'

'You?' echoed Twink weakly, her thoughts spinning. 'But – but Teena, that's not like you at all. I mean –'

'How would *you* know?' demanded her little sister, looking close to tears. 'You've been here at Glitterwings for the last two years! You were always treating me like a baby in acorn school whenever you came home – well, I'm *not*.'

Twink opened her mouth and closed it again. She couldn't speak. She looked at Zuzu, and it felt as if a chasm had opened beneath her feet. Oh, how had she got everything so utterly wrong?

'Zuzu . . . were you really trying to *save* Teena?' she whispered.

The sobbing fairy nodded, and Twink winced, aching inside. 'Oh, Zuzu, I'm so sorry . . .' She reached out to touch the younger fairy's shoulder, but Sooze jerked her cousin away.

'I think you've said enough for now, Twink,' she snapped.

Twink swallowed hard. In a sudden flurry of wings, Miss Twilight and Bimi arrived, and she realised dazedly that not much time had passed since they left Violet Branch. It felt like a lifetime ago.

Miss Twilight took one look at them, and held her hands out to the younger fairies. 'Come along, everyone,' she said. 'I think we all need some hot, sweet nectar.'

To Twink's surprise, not much was said as they sat in Miss Twilight's office. Sooze sat scowling down at her acorn-shell cup. Bimi perched quietly beside Twink, sipping her hot nectar. She rubbed her wing warmly against Twink's, and Twink gave her a grateful smile.

The two younger fairies sat huddled together. The colour slowly returned to their cheeks as they drained their drinks. 'Would – would we really have fallen if Twink and Sooze hadn't arrived?' asked

Teena fearfully.

Miss Twilight nodded. 'Though you wouldn't have fallen very far – there's a protection spell around the railing. Still, it would have been a nasty shock for you, and you might have hurt yourself on one of the branches.'

Twink saw her little sister take a deep breath. 'It was my fault,' she blurted out. 'Zu only came along because she couldn't talk me out of it. Please don't punish her. I'm the one who should be punished!'

Miss Twilight smiled slightly. '*I* shan't be doing any punishing – you're Mrs Lightwing's students, not mine. However, I shall recommend to her that you receive more of a punishment than Zuzu.'

Teena looked relieved. She and Zuzu exchanged a small smile.

'But I'm afraid Mrs Lightwing might want to make an example of you both regardless,' added Miss Twilight. 'You were told at the start of the year that the platform was strictly forbidden!'

'Will they be expelled?' burst out Twink anxiously. 'Oh, please – it wasn't *really* Teena's fault; it was mine! If I hadn't been such a moss brain all term, then this probably wouldn't have happened –'

'I don't think you need to worry about their being expelled,' said Miss Twilight gently, gathering up the cups. 'But there might be quite a bit of window-washing in their futures! Go to bed now, everyone – except for Twink and Sooze. I want to speak to you both.'

Bimi gave Twink a quick, reassuring smile as she left. Teena and Zuzu looked subdued, glancing worriedly behind them as they shut the door.

Miss Twilight sat behind her desk and laced her fingers together. 'There seemed to be some sort of argument going on as I flew up,' she said mildly, looking from Twink to Sooze.

Sooze glowered at the ceiling, tapping her pink wings together.

'Er – yes,' muttered Twink. Then she remembered Teena's earlier frankness, and she squared her shoulders. 'It was my fault,' she said. 'I – I've got everything all wrong this term.'

Miss Twilight listened quietly as Twink told her all

that had happened. After a moment, Sooze stopped frowning at the ceiling and glared at Twink instead. Twink faltered, and soon found herself mumbling her story to the floor.

'You did *what?*' burst out Sooze when Twink described how she'd attempted to get Teena and Summer together. She leapt to her feet, wings trembling. 'I can't believe you tried to stop Zuzu and Teena from being friends!'

Twink glanced at Miss Twilight, but their Star Magic teacher sat without speaking, watching them both carefully. Twink swallowed. 'I know,' she said. 'I was wrong, Sooze. I – I thought Zuzu was just like you, and that Teena might get hurt –'

She stopped in confusion. Sooze looked as if she had just been slapped. 'Oh!' she whispered. 'You mean . . .' Sudden tears sprang to her eyes, and she looked away, hiding her face with her wings.

'Oh, *Sooze*!' gasped Twink, horrified. Sooze, who never cried!

She jumped up, wanting to comfort Sooze in some way, but afraid she'd be rebuffed. 'I – I'm really sorry –' she stammered. 'Sooze, you're one of my best friends now, you know you are! It's just that – you know, our first term together . . .'

Sooze wiped her eyes, and tried to laugh. 'Yeah, I know – I was a real wasp brain back then. Not as big a one as you've been this term, though,' she added fiercely.

Twink nodded. 'I know,' she murmured. 'I was stupid, Sooze, I really was! But – I was only trying to protect Teena.'

Sooze snorted. 'Protect her! Why, Zuzu's one of the nicest fairies I know. Your sister's *lucky* to have her for a friend.'

'I know that now,' said Twink. She put her hand on Sooze's arm. 'I'm really sorry,' she said. 'I'll apologise to Zuzu again, too. Can we still be friends, Sooze? Please?' She held her breath.

Sooze scowled at the wall for a moment, and then sighed and rolled her eyes. 'Oh, I suppose so,' she said. 'I've got used to having you around, Opposite, so we might as well keep on being friends – even if you *do* act like a total moss brain sometimes.'

'Thanks,' said Twink softly, squeezing Sooze's hand. All at once she felt she couldn't have borne it if she and Sooze hadn't been friends any more – she needed her Opposite, in a way that even Bimi couldn't fulfil.

'Good,' said Miss Twilight. Standing up from her desk, she stretched her wings. They glistened like pieces of evening sky.

'I *do* like it when students solve their own problems – it saves me so much work!' she smiled. 'Now get to bed, you two . . . before I remember that you weren't supposed to be up on that platform outside lesson time.'

As Twink and Sooze left Miss Twilight's office, a hissing whisper pierced the air.

'Psst! Twink!'

Twink spun about. 'Teena!' she said in surprise as her little sister emerged from the shadows.

Sooze grinned. 'I'll see you up in Violet Branch, Twink. Looks like you've got some talking to do.'

As Sooze flew away up the trunk, Twink quickly drew Teena over to one of the moonlit windows. 'What are *you* doing here?' she demanded. 'You're supposed to be in bed!'

Teena lifted her chin. 'Well, I'm already in so much trouble that I didn't think it would matter much. And – and besides, I wanted to make sure you were all right.'

Twink's eyes widened. 'Make sure *I'm* all right? But that's what I'm supposed to do with you! I'm the big sister, remember?'

'I'm supposed to look out for you as well,' said Teena firmly. 'That's what sisters do for each other – even if I *am* younger!'

The two fairies gazed at each other in the moonlight. It suddenly hit Twink, hard, what it had taken her all term to work out: Teena was growing up. Her little sister was her own fairy now.

'Yes, I'm all right,' she said in a low voice. 'And Teena . . . I'm really proud of you for speaking up in there. I – I'm proud of you, full stop.'

Teena smiled and ducked her head. From the pink glow of her cheeks, Twink knew that everything was going to be all right between them. Relief flowed through her. She and Teena hugged tightly, fluttering their wings to stay aloft.

'Come on,' said Twink as they pulled apart. She ruffled Teena's long hair. 'I'll fly you up to Snowdrop Branch.'

'OK,' said Teena with a grin.

The two sisters flew side by side up the shadowy trunk. Twink cleared her throat. 'Teena, I – I'm sorry about how I've acted this term,' she said. 'It was stupid of me to dislike Zuzu without knowing her. And trying to get you together with Summer . . .' She shuddered. 'I was such an idiot!'

'Yes, you were,' agreed Teena, bumping against her good-naturedly. 'You're going to love Zuzu when you get to know her! But you know what else, Twink? I think *you* should be friends with Summer – you're the one who likes her so much.'

Twink made a rueful face. 'Why would she want to be friends with me, after how I tricked her? I don't blame her a bit for helping with the prank.'

'She'll forgive you,' said Teena. 'So will Zuzu,' she added, tucking her arm through Twink's.

'Thanks,' whispered Twink. Her little sister seemed so confident that Twink couldn't help believing it herself, and her spirits lifted.

The two fairies fell into silence, drinking in the tree's beauty as they fluttered upwards: the shafts of silvery moonlight angling into the dark trunk, and the flowers hanging over every ledge.

Tipping her head back, Twink thought how lucky she was to go to Glitterwings Academy, the best school in the world – and how much luckier still she was to have Teena for her sister.

Everything will be fine, she thought happily, squeezing her sister's arm. *Just as long as we've got each other!*

Read on
for the glimmery
beginning of Twink's
next adventure

From Treasure Hunt

The sun shone brightly as Twink Flutterby skimmed over summer-green fields with her mother and sister. On such a lovely morning, the journey to Glitterwings Academy should have been the most delightful thing in the world.

Twink hardly noticed it. She cast furtive glances at her mother as they flew. Although Mrs Flutterby was clearly trying to act as if nothing was wrong, she seemed tired and worried. Twink bit her lip, wondering whether she should mention what she had overheard the night before.

Fortunately, Teena was too excited about returning to school to pick up on the mood. 'Oh, I can hardly wait!' she cried, doing a quick somersault in the air. 'Are we almost there, Mum?'

'Almost,' said Twink's mother. 'It's just over this hill.'

'Hurrah!' Teena darted ahead, her wings a lavender blur. A moment later she was back again. 'Mum, I can see Zuzu! . . .'

Titania Woods

There are lots more stories about Glitterwings
Academy – make sure you haven't missed any of them!

If you have any difficulty in finding these in your local bookshop,
please visit www.bloomsbury.com or call 020 7440 2475
to order direct from Bloomsbury Publishing.

Visit www.glitterwingsacademy.co.uk for more fabulous fairy fun!